THE ANIMALS' SANTA

JAN BRETT

THE ANIMALS' SANTA

SCHOLASTIC INC.

For
Brian Stirling Koloski

ISBN 978-0-545-90842-9

12 11 10 9 8 7 6 5 4 3 2 1   15 16 17 18 19 20/0

Printed in the U.S.A.   08

This edition first printing, September 2015

Design by Marikka Tamura
Text set in Golden Cockerel ITC Std
The art for this book was done in watercolors and gouache.
Airbrush backgrounds by Joseph Hearne

"It's your first Christmas Eve, Little Snow.
The animals' Santa comes tonight!" Big Snowshoe
told his little brother.

"Who is the animals' Santa?" Little Snow asked.

"We don't know who he is," Big Snowshoe said.

"Did you ever see him?" Little Snow asked.

"No," the forest animals chimed in.
"But we find presents from him on Christmas."

"Last year, I found a heart-shaped wishing stone on my pillow when I woke up," Big Snowshoe told him.

"I was asleep when I heard *ding-dong, ding-dong.*
I opened my eyes, and this little bell was right there
next to me," the porcupine said.

The raven twins cawed, "A puzzle toy was hanging from our tree branch on Christmas morning."

"We woke up and found a tasty sack of plump acorns," the squirrel cousins chattered.

"Someone left me a brush to fluff my beautiful tail,"
the arctic fox said proudly.
Little Snow hadn't said a word.

"Wouldn't someone have seen his tracks in the snow?"
he asked. "I think you are fooling me."

"No, we aren't," Big Snowshoe said.

He wasn't sure who the animals' Santa might be,
but he believed he would come on Christmas.

"We think he's a badger," the squirrels chattered.
"His thick fur coat keeps him warm in the far north."

"No," the raven twins cawed. "There's always
snow at Christmas and if there is a blizzard,
it would take a polar bear to find his way."

"I'm sure he's a moose," the porcupine told them. "He can plow his way through deep, snowy drifts."

"He could be a wolf," the arctic fox said, smiling.
"There is no animals' Santa," Little Snow shouted,
"and anyone who thinks so is silly."

"I believe there is," Big Snowshoe told him.
But he wished that he had seen the animals'
Santa so he could be really sure.

"No, no, no!" Little Snow thumped his thumper foot so hard, it shattered the ice on the stream. Broken bits slid across in a starburst, making jingly-jangly noises.

What a beautiful sound, Big Snowshoe thought as
he helped his brother up the bank. "It's starting to
feel like Christmas. Let's go home and get warm."

The rabbit family snuggled down for the night.
"Maybe tonight we will see the animals' Santa,"
Big Snowshoe whispered.
"*Snore . . .*" Little Snow mumbled at him and fell asleep.

Big Snowshoe was wide-awake. Suddenly he had an
idea. He crept out of bed and went down to the stream.

Big Snowshoe picked up lacy pieces of broken
ice and carried them home to make ice chimes.
He pulled up strands of hedge grass.

He tied them to the delicate pieces of ice and
hung them from branches. There was no wind,
so the icy pieces stayed still.

It was midnight when a silvery note rang
through the forest, then another and another.
It was Big Snowshoe's ice chimes.

The rabbit family and the other animals woke up
and jumped out of bed. *Is it the animals' Santa?* they
wondered.

The animals did not see anyone or
any tracks in the snow.

Then, as if falling from the moon, a bundle
of sweet clover landed at their feet.

The animals looked up as one gift after another fell from the sky. Were they from the animals' Santa?

A white shape flew silently above them.
Little Snow shrugged. "It's only a bird," he said.

As if he had heard, the snowy owl turned back
and called out, "Merry Christmas, little friends."

"Everyone! Look!" Little Snow pointed at the sky.
"It's the animals' Santa!"

Little Snow waved at the snowy owl and whispered
into the night, "Animals' Santa, now I know that you are
truly, truly, true."